WHO IS HERMAN?

He's the guy next door, the bum who fixed your car, your brother-in-law—he's everybody and nobody. And you can even recognize yourself in him as he plods through life's ups and downs in his own odd-ball way. So turn the page and join the fun with Herman and his friends.

"Where's the kids, Herman?"

⊘ SIGNET (04

MORE BIG LAUGHſ

☐ **MARMADUKE SOUNDS OFF** by Brad Anderson. (136756—$1.9
☐ **MARMADUKE: TAKE 2** by Brad Anderson. (132874—$1.9
☐ **"WHERE'S THE KIDS, HERMAN?"** by Jim Unger. (129229—$1.9
☐ **"APART FROM A LITTLE DAMPNESS, HERMAN, HOW'S EVERYTHING ELSⱲ**
by Jim Unger. (127811—$1.9
☐ **"AND YOU WONDER, HERMAN, WHY I NEVER GO TO ITALIAN RESTAURANT**
by Jim Unger. (135458—$1.9
☐ **"IN ONE OF YOUR MOODS AGAIN, HERMAN?"** by Jim Unger.
(134958—$1.9⁚
☐ **"ANY OTHER COMPLAINTS, HERMAN?"** by Jim Unger. (136322—$1.9⁚
☐ **"NOW WHAT ARE YOU UP TO, HERMAN?"** by Jim Unger.(138236—$1.9
☐ **IT'S HARD TO BE HIP OVER THIRTY** by Judith Viorst. (131320—$1.9
☐ **PEOPLE & OTHER AGGRAVATIONS** by Judith Viorst. (113667—$1.⁚
☐ **BORED OF THE RINGS, OR TOLKIEN REVISITED** by National Lampoⁿ
(137302—$2.5◉
☐ **A DIRTY BOOK** by National Lampoon. (132254—$2.9⁚
☐ **MORE FUNNY LAWS** by Earle and Jim Harvey. (135822—$1.9⁚

*Prices slightly higher in Canada

Buy them at your local bookstore or use this convenient coupon for ordering

NEW AMERICAN LIBRARY,
P.O. Box 999, Bergenfield, New Jersey 07621

Please send me the books I have checked above. I am enclosing $_____
(please add $1.00 to this order to cover postage and handling). Send che
or money order—no cash or C.O.D.'s Prices and numbers are subject to chan
without notice

Name _____

Address_____

City_____ State_____ Zip Code_____
Allow 4-6 weeks for delivery.
This offer is subject to withdrawal without notice.

"Where's the kids, Herman?"

by Jim Unger

A SIGNET BOOK

NEW AMERICAN LIBRARY

0NAL BOOKS ARE AVAILABLE AT QUANTITY DISCOUNTS WHEN USED TO
PROMOTE PRODUCTS OR SERVICES. FOR INFORMATION PLEASE WRITE TO
PREMIUM MARKETING DIVISION, NEW AMERICAN LIBRARY,
1633 BROADWAY, NEW YORK, NEW YORK 10019.

Copyright © 1978, 1979, 1984 by Universal Press Syndicate

All rights reserved. No part of this book may be used or
reproduced in any manner whatsoever without written permission
except in the case of reprints in the context of reviews.
For information write Andrews, McMeel & Parker, Inc.,
a Universal Press Syndicate Company,
4400 Johnson Drive, Fairway, Kansas 66205.

Published by arrangement with Andrews, McMeel & Parker Inc., a Unive
Press Syndicate Company.

''Herman is syndicated internationally by
UNIVERSAL PRESS SYNDICATE

SIGNET TRADEMARK REG. U.S. PAT. OFF. AND FOREIGN COUNTRIES
REGISTERED TRADEMARK—MARCA REGISTRADA
HECHO EN WINNIPEG, CANADA

SIGNET, SIGNET CLASSIC, MENTOR, PLUME, MERIDIAN AND
NAL BOOKS are published by New American Library,
1633 Broadway, New York, New York 10019

First Signet Printing, May, 1984

4   5   6   7   8   9

PRINTED IN CANADA

"Okay, now shift your weight onto the left leg during the follow-through."

"You're not allowed to be a grandfather anymore; you're a 'grandperson.'"

"Hey Mom. I got that job. Get over here quick and show me what to do."

"It wasn't THAT under-cooked."

"We're gonna have supper as soon as you shove off."

"He's a self-made man."

"You've got an hour to paint your nails and an hour to talk to your mother. I'm going to a meeting."

"Do you have to keep saying 'bunch of junk'
every five minutes. I'm enjoying it!"

"Of course I care for you. Money and looks aren't everything you know!"

"QUIT SHOVING!"

"Whaddyer mean 'checkmate'? Get to bed."

"See that! I forgot to tighten the nut."

"Debbie looks exactly like me when I was 18."

"D'yer like that blue?"

"I thought I'd put in a little vegetable garden."

"This is Blue Buzzard, good buddy; Smokey's on the warpath."

"There...now argue!"

"I haven't got those in a twelve but I can let you have a couple of pair of size sixes."

"Maybe you're beginning to get the message that
we need a recreation room."

"Don't look at me like that, I was polishing it."

"How long have you had your feet on the wrong legs?"

"I see you've listed your hobbies as alpine skiing, scuba, sky-diving, treasure hunting and climbing Mount Everest."

"Congratulations! He seems very bright."

"Well, if you didn't rob the bank, how are
you gonna pay my fee to prove your
innocence?"

"Did you say this pizza gave you indigestion?"

"We can't live with my parents. They're still
living with their parents!"

"I decided to come in today. The poolroom's packed."

"I'll leave you to park the car, I'm going to bed."

"If I can't get a summer job this year I think
I'll get married."

"Why don't you let your husband go
to the ball game?"

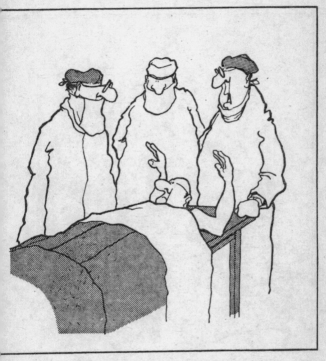

"He thinks we're muggers!"

"All the clocks have stopped!"

"I told you he wouldn't eat that ice cream."

"I cut a piece off the bottom and patched your shi[rt...]"

"I know the same thing happened last year. I'm 'accident prone.'"

"I'll be home soon; I'm at the Speedy
Shoe Repair Boutique."

"That pain-in-the-neck's out here, doctor."

"I'll count to three, then I'm gonna use the sink."

"Don't forget to mark it 'Personal.'"

"Aren't you going to phone the airport?"

"When we say 'parents invited' we usually mean
to sit and watch."

"That was a good idea, sending out for a pizza
while the elevator's on the fritz."

"It was supposed to be Mom, but I messed it up."

"Try to imagine how much I care!"

"His English teacher says he's a groovy, far-out kid."

"It just says, 'Windows repaired—five bucks.'"

"You must have run a mile this time—you've been gone four minutes."

"Don't go rushing into marriage. Look around for a couple of years like your mother did."

"I warned you about iron tonic. Your stomach's rusty."

"Does that hurt?"

"If you remember, I did mention possible
side-effects."

"Good King Wen-ces-las looked out...on the
feast of Steeeephen..."

"How come I get a different driving
instructor every week?"

"I've had a hard day, so don't make any smart remarks while I'm carrying a cream pie."

"Don't move while I'm gone. You'll spill
my drink."

"Grannie, your horoscope says be prepared for a
whirlwind romance!"

"You got nothing to smile about."

"Butcher Harris is doing this one
tomorrow morning."

"If you only want to spend five dollars, I'd recommend two hamburgers and a three buck tip."

CASHIER

"I haven't understood one word you said. Come back when your face gets better."

"That bit about 'Love, honor and obey.' Is that me or her?"

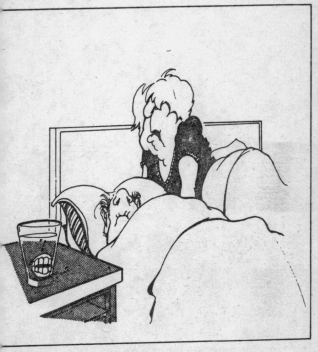

"I hope you used warm water. I don't want to
listen to those things chattering all night."

"Okay, you've got your 'nose job.' Now get out there and meet girls."

"'F' means 'fantastic.'"

"The sink's backed up!"

"I'm NOT going camping. If you wanna get back to nature, take the bug screen out of the window for half an hour."

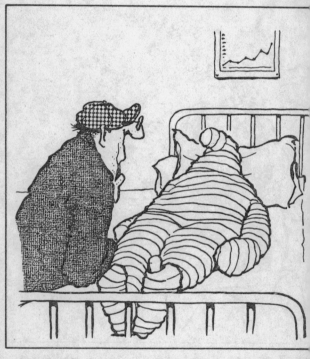

"Herm, want me to make a little hole and feed
you some qrapes?"

"Fifteen years is not so long. You've already done 12 days."

"You're looking at it upside down!"

"You're washing the floor with tomorrow's soup-of-the-day!"

"Hey lady! If you keep your rollers lined up with
the screen, I'll be able to watch the movie."

"Don't say 'so what' when I tell you your foot's on fire."

"I'm just showing these guys around the place."

"Guess what Mike does for a living!"

"I guess we should have tried it on the rats first."

"You're the one guy we can trust in this cell for a couple of days 'til we get those bars fixed."

"The bottom's dropped out of the market.
I've lost 18 bucks."

"It's been postponed. He's got a headache."

"I can get a court order to stop you from teaching her to cook."

"Mom, why don't you get a divorce and marry someone with more money?"

"We implant this behind your left ear and you won't even know it's there."

"How was Africa?"

"I know you've been late for work twice this week.
I still think it's stupid to sleep in the car!"

"I know you want to play Hamlet, but for this one television commercial you're a stick of celery."

"No, you can't wear it to school. Put it back on the wall."

"I am grateful! But I distinctly remember
asking for a cheese sandwich."

"Herman fixed the washer!"

"I've unclogged the upstairs bath."

"So you dyed your hair and it turned green. You can't spend the rest of your life in this bathroom."

"Keep out! Keep out! K-E-E-P O-U-T."

ABOUT THE AUTHOR

JIM UNGER was born in London, England. After surviving the blitz bombings of World War II and two years in the British Army, followed by a short career as a London bobby and a driving instructor, he immigrated to Canada in 1968, where he became a newspaper graphic artist and editorial cartoonist. For three years running he won the Ontario Weekly Newspaper Association's "Cartoonist of the Year" award. In 1974 he began drawing HERMAN for Universal Press Syndicate, with instant popularity. HERMAN is now enjoyed by 60 million daily and Sunday newspaper readers all around the world. His cartoon collections, THE HERMAN TREASURIES, became paperback bestsellers.

Jim Unger now lives in Nassau, Bahamas.